LONGMAN CLASSICS

King Solomon's Mines

Sir H Rider Haggard

Simplified by D K Swan
and Michael West
Illustrated by Mark Peppé

LONGMAN

Addison Wesley Longman Limited,
Edinburgh Gate, Harlow,
Essex CM20 2JE, England
and Associated Companies throughout the world.

This simplified edition © Longman Group UK Limited 1989

*All rights reserved; no part of this publication
may be reproduced, stored in a retrieval system,
or transmitted in any form or by any means, electronic,
mechanical, photocopying, recording, or otherwise,
without the prior written permission of the Publishers.*

First published in 1991
Ninth impression 1996

ISBN 0-582-01821-8

Set in 10/13 point Linotron 202 Versailles
Printed in China
GCC/09

Acknowledgements

The cover background is a wallpaper design called NUAGE,
courtesy of Osborne and Little plc.

Stage 4: 1800 word vocabulary

Please look under *New words* at the back of this book
for explanations of words outside this stage.

Contents

Introduction

Sir H Rider Haggard

Rider Haggard was born in England in 1856. At the age of nineteen he went to South Africa as secretary to the governor of Natal. He held other official positions and ended his South African experience as the manager of an ostrich farm (at a time when no European lady of importance could be without an ostrich feather in at least one of her hats).

In 1881 he returned to England to study law. He completed his studies and became a barrister in 1884, but he did not practise very often in the law courts. Instead he travelled in many countries and served on a large number of committees, especially official committees dealing with farming and country matters. His interest in rural affairs expressed itself in books like *A Farmer's Year* (1899), *Rural England* (1902) and *The Poor and the Land* (1905) and in a good many articles for newspapers and magazines.

But he became famous (and rich) as the result of his novels of African adventure: *King Solomon's Mines* (1885), *Allan Quatermain* (1887), *She* (1887), and *Ayesha, or the Return of She* (1905). These are still considered to be classics of their kind.

Altogether, Haggard wrote about fifty novels, mostly adventure stories. He was not what we would call a full-time writer of fiction, since he never stopped his work of public service. It was a remarkable output.

King Solomon

King Solomon was the third king of Israel from about 972 BC to 922. He was the son of King David and Bathsheba. The story of his success as a king, his wisdom and his riches is told in the Bible (1 Kings 2–11; 2 Chronicles 1–9) and in other books.

In those accounts there are descriptions of his trading with distant countries, and there has always been guess-work about where those countries were. Some people believed that the Queen of Sheba, who visited King Solomon in Jerusalem, came from Africa, perhaps from Ethiopia. Others placed in southern Africa the port or country of Ophir, which sent gold and precious stones to Solomon. So it seemed reasonable for Rider Haggard to imagine Solomon's diamond mines somewhere north of where Zimbabwe is today. (We now believe that Sheba and Ophir were both in southern Arabia, Sheba perhaps in what is now Yemen, and Ophir perhaps the Dhofar province of Oman.)

Precious stones are mentioned in 1 Kings 1:10: "Hiram's fleet of ships, which had brought gold from Ophir, brought in also from Ophir cargoes of almug wood and precious stones." We read, too, that Solomon had his own fleet of ships, and they came home to ports on the Red Sea once every three years. That suggests that they went quite far away, using the monsoon winds out and back. The monsoon winds blow from the north-east during the winter months and from the south-west during the summer months. That means that the north-east winds would help the ships to sail south during the winter months. They would trade during the next twelve months, and then return, using the south-west monsoon to help them.

Southern Africa

In the 1880s, travel in southern Africa was very slow. There were very few roads, and for a journey like that described in Chapter 3, white men used heavy wagons pulled by cattle – several pairs, with one man, a "leader", finding the way for the first pair, and a "driver" making all the cattle pull.

Cattle couldn't be taken into the areas where there were tsetse fly. And that is why the hero and his friends had to leave the wagon at Inyati and continue their journey on foot.

The Zulu tribe became very powerful under certain chiefs like Shaka in the nineteenth century. There were a number of occasions when Zulu armies fought against the white men who were spreading over southern Africa. Readers may have seen films about Africa at that time that show the well-trained Zulu companies in action. This is the kind of force Rider Haggard imagines in his "Kukuanaland".

Chapter 1
I meet Sir Henry Curtis

It is a curious thing that at the age of fifty-five I should be trying to write a history.

Did you ever hear of the Suliman Mountains? That is where King Solomon had his diamond mines. An old woman up in the Manica country told me about it many years ago. She said that the people who lived across those mountains were a branch of the Zulu people, speaking a language rather like the Zulu language. They were finer and bigger even than the Zulus. She said that powerful witches lived among them, and these witches had the secret of a wonderful mine of "bright stones".

I laughed at the story at the time. But twenty years later, I learnt something more about the Suliman Mountains and the country beyond them. I was up at a place called Sitanda's Kraal when a Portuguese man arrived. He told me that his name was José Silvestre. I was able to help him in a few ways. When he left, he said:

"Goodbye. If ever we meet again, I'll be the richest man in the world."

Two weeks later, he came back from the desert. He was carried into my camp by two of my hunters. His lips were cracked, and his tongue was black. I did my best for him, but he was dying. When he was able to speak in a very faint voice, the next day, I heard:

"Listen, friend. I am dying, I know. You have been good to me, so I will give you the writing. Perhaps you will get there if you can live to cross the desert."

He felt inside his shirt and brought out a bit of torn yellow cloth with something written on it in red-brown

1

letters. With it was a piece of paper and a map.

His voice was growing weaker as he said: "The paper gives what is written on the cloth. It took me years to read it. I am the descendant of a José da Silvestre, who lived three hundred years ago. He wrote it when he was dying on those mountains. His slave found him dead and brought the writing back. It has been in the family ever since."

He died soon after that. I have had the writing translated into English:

I am José da Silvestre. I am dying of hunger in a little cave on the north side of the mountain which I have called Sheba's Breasts. The cave is in the southern of the two mountains. I write this in the year 1590. My pen is a piece of bone, my paper is a piece of cloth torn from my shirt, and I am writing with my own blood. If my slave finds this when he comes, he will bring it to Delagoa, to my friend ... [The name cannot be read.] My friend should tell the king what I am going to write, so that he may send an army. If the army can live through the desert and conquer the people, the Kukuanas, he will become the richest king on earth. With my own eyes I have seen millions of diamonds stored in Solomon's Treasure Room behind the White Death. But Gagool, the witch, deceived me, and I brought nothing away, scarcely my life. He who comes must follow the map and climb the snow of Sheba's left breast until he reaches the top. On the north side of that lies the great road that Solomon made. From there it is three days' journey to the king's palace. He must kill Gagool.

José da Silvestre

2

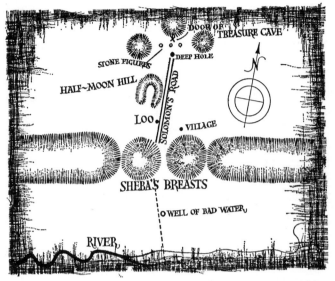

José da Silvestre's map

Eighteen months ago, I met Sir Henry Curtis and Captain Good. They were on a ship on which I was travelling to my home in Durban. Sir Henry was the largest and strongest-looking man I ever saw. He had yellow hair, a thick yellow beard, and large grey eyes. I never saw a finer looking man.

Captain John Good had recently left the navy. He was broad, with dark hair, and was rather a curious man to look at. He was so clean, so polished, and he always wore an eyeglass in his right eye. It seemed to grow there: it had no string, and he never took it out in daylight except to clean it. He put it in his pocket when he went to bed, together with his teeth. (He had lost his real teeth, and he had had a very fine set of false teeth made to take their place.)

3

At dinner on the ship I was at the same table as these two men. The Captain and I soon started talking about shooting, and after some time he began to talk about elephants.

"Ah," called out somebody who was sitting near me, "you've got the right man for that: Hunter Quatermain can tell you about elephants if any man can."

Sir Henry, who had been listening to our talk, looked surprised. He leaned forward and said in a deep voice, "Pardon me, but is your name Allan Quatermain?"

"Yes."

As we were leaving the dinner table, Sir Henry asked if he and Captain Good could talk to me. We found somewhere to sit, and he began:

"Mr Quatermain, the year before last, you were, I believe, at a place called Bamangwato to the north of the Transvaal."

"I was." I wondered how he knew.

"Did you meet a man called Neville there?"

"Oh, yes. He stopped just beside me for a few weeks to rest his cattle before going on. I had a letter a few months ago, asking me if I knew what had happened to him. I answered it as well as I could at the time."

"Yes," said Sir Henry, "your letter was sent on to me. You said in it that Neville left Bamangwato at the beginning of May in a wagon with a driver and a hunter called Jim, with the intention of going to Inyati. There he meant to sell his wagon and go on foot. You also said that he did sell his wagon, because six months later you saw a trader with the wagon, and he told you that he had bought it at Inyati from a white man, and that he believed the white man, with one servant, had started off on a shooting trip."

"Yes."

4

There was a pause.

Sir Henry said suddenly, "I suppose you know nothing more of the reason for my – for Neville's journey?"

I was silent for a moment. Then: "I think he was starting for Solomon's mines."

"Solomon's mines!" cried both my hearers at once. "Where are they?"

"I don't know," I said. "I know where they are said to be. Once I saw the mountains that defend them, but there were two hundred kilometres of desert between me and them, and I don't know that any white man ever got across it – except one. Perhaps the best thing I can do is to tell you the story of Solomon's mines as I know it."

I told them the story of Silvestre, and because I trusted them, I showed them the map and the translation of the Portuguese note.

"And now," I said, "you want to know about Neville."

"He is – or was – my brother," said Sir Henry.

"Thank you," I said. "I knew the man Jim who was with your brother. He was a man from Bechuanaland, a good hunter, and an unusually clever man. It was he who told me that they were going to find diamonds."

"Mr Quatermain," said Sir Henry, "I'm going to look for my brother till I find him, or until I know that he's dead. Will you come with me? If by chance we find diamonds, they will belong to you and Good equally: I don't want them. Of course, I will pay all the cost and you'll have what you ask as our guide."

I thought for a minute. "Yes," I said. "I'll go. I tell you plainly that I don't think we shall come out of it alive – that is, if we attempt to cross the Suliman Mountains."

Sir Henry's face did not change. "We must take our chance," he said.

Good, Sir Henry and Quatermain on the ship

Chapter 2
Umbopa

When we reached Durban, Sir Henry and Captain Good came and stayed at my house there.

I then bought a wagon and Zulu cattle to pull it. We took ten guns and three pistols.

We decided to take five men – a driver, a leader, and three others. I found the driver and the leader, but to get the three others was more difficult. They had to be thoroughly trustworthy and brave men. At last I obtained two – Ventvogel, an excellent hunter, and Khiva, a young Zulu who knew some English. I looked for the fifth man, but without success. So we decided to start without one.

The evening before our start, Khiva came and told me that a Zulu named Umbopa was waiting to see me. I told Khiva to bring him in. A tall fine-looking man entered, about thirty years old. He sat down on the floor in the corner and remained silent. It seemed to me that his face was familiar.

"I've seen your face before," I said.

"Yes. The chief saw my face at the place of the Little Hand on the day before the battle."

Then I remembered. I was one of Lord Chelmsford's guides in that unfortunate Zulu war. On the day before the battle I was talking to this man, who had command of some friendly Africans. He told me that he had doubts of the safety of the camp. I told him to leave such things to wiser heads; but afterwards I thought of his words.

"I remember," I said. "What is it you want?"

"I hear that you are going on a journey far into the

north with the white chiefs from over the water. Is it true?"

"It is."

"I hear that you are going a month's journey beyond the Manica country. I would like to travel with you. I want no money, but I am a brave man and worth my place and meat."

In some way this man was different from other Zulus, and I did not quite trust his offer to come without pay. I told Sir Henry and Good what he had said, and asked them their opinion.

Sir Henry told me to ask him to stand up. Umbopa did so, at the same time slipping off the long coat he wore, and standing naked except for the cloth round his waist and a string of lions' teeth round his neck. Certainly he was a very fine-looking man. Standing nearly two metres tall, he was broad and well shaped. In that light his skin did not seem dark, except here and there, where deep black lines marked old spear wounds. Sir Henry walked up to him and looked into his proud, fine face.

"They make a good pair, don't they?" said Good.

"I like your looks, Mr Umbopa, and I will take you as my servant," said Sir Henry in English.

Umbopa seemed to understand him, for he answered in Zulu, "It is good." And then he added, with a look at the white man's great height and strength, "We are men, you and I."

Chapter 3
Sitanda's Kraal

Now I do not intend to describe our long journey up to Sitanda's Kraal, nearly five thousand kilometres from Durban. We had to go the last five hundred kilometres on foot because of the tsetse fly, whose bite is death to all animals except man and donkeys.

We left Durban at the end of January, and it was in the second week of May that we camped near Sitanda's Kraal.

We left the wagon and the cattle at Inyati in charge of our driver and leader. Then, with Umbopa, Khiva, Ventvogel and half a dozen men we hired to carry our things, we started out on foot on our wild journey from there to Sitanda's Kraal.

We met some wild elephants on the way. One of them charged towards Good. He fell in front of it, and we thought for a moment that his end was certain. But Khiva turned and threw his spear straight in the elephant's face. It struck his trunk. With a cry of pain the beast seized the poor Zulu, and placing a foot on his body, tore him in two! We rushed up and fired again and again, until the elephant fell.

Good rose from the ground. He was very sad about the brave man who had given his life to save him. Umbopa stood gazing at the huge dead elephant and the remains of poor Khiva.

"Ah, well," he said at last, "he is dead; but he died like a man."

We marched on again, and at last we reached Sitanda's Kraal.

Khiva saves Good from the elephant

It was evening. I left Good to see to the arrangements of our little camp, and took Sir Henry with me. We walked to the top of the slope opposite, and gazed across the desert. The air was very clear, and far far away I could see the faint blue form of the Suliman Mountains.

"There," I said, "there is the wall round Solomon's mines, but God knows if we will ever climb it."

"My brother should be there, and, if he is, I'll reach him somehow," said Sir Henry in a voice of calm certainty.

"I hope so," I answered, and turned to go back to the camp. Then I saw that we were not alone. Behind us, also gazing at the far-off mountains, stood Umbopa.

"Is that the land where you want to go?" he said, pointing towards the mountains with his broad spear.

"Yes, Umbopa," answered Sir Henry.

"The desert is wide and there is no water in it; the mountains are high and covered with snow. And man cannot say what lies behind them in the place where the sun rises. It is a long journey."

"Yes," answered Sir Henry, "it is far. I am going to find my brother. And there is no journey on this earth that a man cannot make if he sets his heart on it."

"Great words, my father," answered Umbopa. "Perhaps I too will find a brother over the mountains."

I looked at him. "What do you mean? What do you know about those mountains?"

"A little, a very little. There is a strange land over there, a land of witches and beautiful things; a land of brave people, and of trees, and streams, and snow mountains, and a great white road. I have heard of it."

Chapter 4
Into the desert

Next day we made our arrangements for starting.

We took with us five guns, three pistols, five water-bottles, twelve kilograms of sun-dried meat, our knives, a compass, some matches, and a few other articles.

For a good hunting-knife each, three men from the village agreed to come with us for the first thirty kilometres, each carrying a large pot of water. My aim in this was to fill up our water-bottles again after the first night's march.

We started in the cool of the evening.

We had nothing to guide us except the distant mountains and old José da Silvestre's map. If we failed to find the "Well of bad water" that his map showed in the middle of the desert, we should probably die of thirst.

On we marched silently as shadows through the night and in the heavy sand. It was very quiet and we felt very much alone there in the desert.

At last sunrise came and about an hour later we saw some rocks rising out of the plain. One large rock, hanging out from the others, gave a very pleasant shelter from the heat of the sun. We drank some water and ate a piece of sun-dried meat. Then we lay down and were soon asleep.

It was three o'clock in the afternoon before we woke. We found the water-carriers preparing to return: they had seen enough of the desert already, and no number of knives or other gifts would have made them come a step farther. So we each took a big drink, filled up our water-

12

bottles and then watched them depart on their march home. At half-past four we also started.

At sunset we stopped and waited for the moon to rise; then we marched on through the night until the sun appeared. We drank a little, then lay down on the sand to sleep. There was no shelter. I don't know how we lived through the day. At about three in the afternoon we decided that we could bear it no longer, and we began to move forward again.

At sunset we rested and got some sleep. When the moon rose, we marched on again. We were suffering terribly from thirst. We had not the strength left in us to speak.

At two o'clock we stopped near a little hill. Driven to it by our dreadful thirst, we drank our last drops of water. Then we lay down.

Just as I was dropping off to sleep, I heard Umbopa say to himself, "If we cannot find water, we will all be dead before the moon rises tomorrow."

Chapter 5
Water! Water!

After two hours I woke up. The others were just beginning to wake.

"If we can trust Silvestre's map, there should be some water near here," I said. No one seemed interested in this: it was clear that we could have little faith in the map.

It was growing light. I saw Ventvogel walking about. Then he lifted his nose and seemed to smell the air.

"I smell water," he said.

Just then the sun came up in glory. There, not more than fifty miles away, we saw Sheba's Breasts, and stretching away for hundreds of miles on each side of them was the great Suliman Range.

Sir Henry stroked his yellow beard thoughtfully. "Perhaps there's water on the top of the hill," he said.

We climbed up the sandy sides of the little hill – and sure enough, there, in a deep cut, was water!

We drank, and filled our water-bottles, and started off at once as soon as the moon rose.

Our water was again finished when we reached the foot of the mountain. By good fortune we found some fruit growing in a hollow some way up the mountain side.

As we climbed higher up the mountain, we suffered terribly during the nights from cold.

We had little strength left. Our food was gone.

It was the twenty-third of May. We struggled slowly up the slope of snow, lying down from time to time to rest. At sunset we found ourselves just below Sheba's left breast.

The sun rises over the Suliman Mountains

"I say," said Good, "we ought to be somewhere near the cave that the old gentleman wrote about."

"Yes," I said, "if there is a cave. And if we don't find it before dark, we are dead men."

We marched on in silence. Then Umbopa stopped.

"Look!" he said.

I saw what seemed to be a hole in the snow.

"It is the cave," said Umbopa.

We hurried to the spot, and found that the hole was the mouth of a cave. Just as we reached shelter, the sun went down.

We crept into the cave, and sat close together so as to be warmer. We could not sleep; the cold was too terrible.

At last the air began to grow grey with light. The sun looked in on our half-frozen forms – and also on Ventvogel sitting there among us, dead.

And ... sitting at the end of the cave, I saw another form; the head rested on its breast, and the long arms hung down.

The body was frozen quite stiff.

"José da Silvestre, of course," said Good.

"Impossible!" I cried. "He died three hundred years ago."

"Why not? What is there to prevent him from lasting for three thousand years, frozen hard as he is? Look, here is the 'piece of bone' that he drew the map with."

"Yes," said Sir Henry, "and here is the place where he got the blood to draw it with," and he pointed to a small wound on the left arm of the body.

We left those two, Silvestre and poor Ventvogel, and crept out of the cave into the sunshine. We wondered how many hours it would be before we were like them.

Chapter 6
Solomon's Road

We walked to the edge of the mountain. The mist had cleared a little. Below us, at the end of a long slope of snow, we saw some green grass, through which a stream was running. By the stream stood a group of large deer. There was plenty of food if we could only get it.

Good and I aimed very carefully, and fired. As the smoke cleared away we saw a great animal lying on its back. We would not die for want of food.

As we ate, our life and strength seemed to come back to us. We began to look about us. Two thousand feet below us lay a great area of the most beautiful country I have ever seen. Here was a thick forest, and there a great river went on its silvery way. To the left lay rich grass-land on which we could see numberless cattle. To the right were hills, with fields of grain between them.

We sat and gazed in silence at this wonderful view. Then Sir Henry spoke.

"That must be Solomon's great road," he said.

It was a splendid road cut out of the rock, at least fifteen metres wide, and kept in good order.

We made our way down to the road and marched along it.

At midday we came to a wood and a small stream. We had a meal and rested. After some time I noticed that Good was not there. But then I saw him sitting by the bank of the stream in which he had been bathing. He had on only his shirt. He was brushing his clothes, shaking his head sadly at the many torn places. Then he polished his shoes. Next he began to brush his hair very carefully. Suddenly I saw a flash of light that passed by his head.

Good sprang up with a curse, and so did I. A group of men had come from among the trees.

They were very tall. Some of them wore black feathers on their heads and had short coats of skins. In front of them stood a youth of about seventeen. His hand was still raised: it was he who had thrown the spear. As I looked, an old soldier-like man stepped forward, and caught the youth by the arm, and said something to him. Then they came towards us.

Sir Henry and Good seized their guns. The men still came on: it seemed to me that they did not know what guns were.

"Put down your guns!" I shouted to the others. Walking forward, I addressed the man who had spoken to the spear-thrower.

"Greeting," I said in Zulu, not knowing what language to use. To my surprise, I was understood.

"Greeting," answered the man, speaking in Zulu, but in an ancient form of the language. "Where have you come from? Why are the faces of three of you white, and the face of the fourth like our faces?" At this he pointed to Umbopa. I saw that the face of Umbopa was like the faces of the men in front of me.

"We are strangers, and come in peace," I answered.

"You lie," he replied, "for no strangers can cross the mountains. But what do your lies matter? You must die, for no strangers may live in the land of the Kukuanas. It is the king's law. Prepare to die, strangers."

I saw the hands of some of the men move down to the great knives at their sides.

"O Lord!" murmured Good; and, as he often did when he was anxious, he put his hand to his false teeth, pulled down the upper set and allowed them to fly back with a crack. It was a most fortunate move: the Kukuanas gave a shout of terror and ran back some distance.

"What's the matter?" I wondered.

"It's his teeth," whispered Sir Henry excitedly. "He moved them. Take them out, Good!"

Good obeyed, hiding the set in his hand.

The men advanced slowly – eager and yet afraid. It seemed that they had now forgotten their intention of killing us.

"How is it, strangers," asked the old man, pointing to Good, who had on him nothing but his shoes and a shirt, "how is it that this fat man has his body clothed but his legs bare, that he has one shining eye, and has teeth that move?"

"Open your mouth," I said to Good. Good curled up his lips and showed a mouth as toothless as that of a new-born babe.

"Where are his teeth?" they shouted.

Good passed his hand across his mouth: then he opened his lips again, and there were two rows of lovely teeth.

Now the young man who had cast the spear gave a howl of terror.

"I see that you are not human," said the old man. "Did ever man born of woman have a round shining eye, or teeth that moved, and melted away, and grew again! Pardon us, my lords."

"We come from another world," I said, "though we are men like you. We come from the biggest star that shines at night."

"Oh! Oh!" they cried in wonder.

"We have come to stay with you for a time, and to bless you. Now, what should we do to the one who threw a spear at Him-whose-teeth-come-and-go?"

"Spare him, my lords," said the old man. "He is the king's son."

"Perhaps," I said, "you doubt our power to kill him? You!" I cried to Umbopa, "give me the magic pipe that speaks."

Umbopa handed me a gun.

"You see that deer," I said, pointing to an animal standing near a rock about seventy metres away. "Tell me, is it possible for a man to kill it from here with a noise?"

"It is not possible, my lord," answered the old man. I raised the gun.

Crack! The deer fell on the rock – dead.

"We are satisfied," said the old man. "All the witches of our people cannot do a thing like that. Listen, Children of the Stars, Children of the Shining Eye and Vanishing Teeth, who roar in thunder and kill from far away. I am Infadoos, son of Kafa, who was once king of the Kukuana people. This youth is Scragga, son of Twala, the great king, lord of the Kukuanas, keeper of the Great Road, terror of his enemies, leader of a hundred thousand soldiers, Twala the One-eyed, the Black, the Terrible."

"Is that so?" I said carelessly. "Lead us, then, to Twala. We do not talk with low people."

The old man made a deep bow and murmured the words, "Koom, Koom," which I afterwards discovered to be their royal greeting. He then turned and addressed his followers. They took all our things to carry them for us – except the guns, which they would not touch.

Chapter 7
We enter Kukuanaland

"Infadoos," I said as we walked, "who made this road?"

"It was made, my lord, in ancient times. None know how or when, not even the wise woman, Gagool, who has lived for hundreds of years."

"Has the king many soldiers?" I asked.

"When Twala the king calls up his companies, they cover the plain."

"Has there been any war lately?"

"There was a war years ago amongst ourselves."

"How was that?"

"It is our custom that, when two sons are born at the same time, the weaker must die. The king, years ago, had two sons born together. Kafa was the stronger. Everyone thought that Twala, the weaker, was dead. Kafa became king. When he died, his oldest son, Imoltu, was made king. But Gagool, the wise and terrible woman, lead out Twala, whom she had hidden. Twala killed Imotu, but Imotu's wife escaped with her new-born child, Ignosi; and nobody has seen her since."

"Then, if this child, Ignosi, had lived, he would be the true king of the Kukuana people?" I said.

"Yes. The eldest son of the king is marked at birth by the Creeping Beast round his waist. We would know him by that. If he is alive, he is king: but he must be dead."

Umbopa was walking just behind me, listening with great interest.

A message had gone ahead of us. In the early afternoon we reached a village. As we drew near we saw company after company of men marching out from its gates. It was a splendid sight to see them. They charged swiftly up the rising ground towards us with flashing spears and waving feathers, and made a line on each side of the road. There they stood as if made of iron until we were opposite to them. Then, at a sign given by the commanding officer, the royal greeting, "Koom!" came from hundreds of throats.

These men were "The Greys" from the colour of their shields. They were the finest soldiers of the Kukuana nation, and Infadoos was their leader.

As soon as we had passed, the Greys formed up behind us and followed us, marching in our rear with a regular step that shook the ground.

At sunset, from the top of some hills, we saw the city of Loo, capital of Kukuanaland. It was a very large place, eight kilometres round. Near it was a curious hill shaped like a half-moon. A hundred kilometres beyond it rose three strangely shaped snow-capped mountains.

Infadoos saw us looking at these mountains and said, "The road ends there. The mountains are full of caves. It is there that the wise men of old time used to go to get whatever it was that they came to this country for. It is there now that our dead kings are laid in the Place of Death."

In an hour's time we reached the edge of the town. We came to a great gate. Infadoos gave some word, and we passed through into the main street.

He led us past endless lines of huts to the gate of a group of huts. We were glad to eat and then sleep, very weary after our long journey.

Chapter 8
Twala the king

When we woke, the sun was high in the heavens. In-fadoos came to say that Twala the king was ready to see us.

We took our guns, and some presents for the king and walked a few hundred metres to a very large courtyard. It was filled by many companies of soldiers – seven or eight thousand.

The space in front of a large hut was empty, but facing it there were several seats. At a sign from Infadoos, we sat down.

At last the door of the hut opened and a huge man stepped out, followed by the boy, Scragga, and what looked like a dried-up monkey in a fur coat. The king sat down, and Scragga stood behind him. The "dried-up monkey" crept on all four feet into the shade of the hut and sat down.

There was silence.

Then the king stood up. He had the most entirely evil and terrible face we had ever seen. He had one fierce black eye; the other eye had gone and there was only a hollow in the face where it had been. The look of the face was altogether cruel, and bad in every way. From his head rose a number of white feathers. His body was covered with shining armour. In his right hand was a huge spear. On his forehead shone a huge diamond.

Still there was silence; but not for long. The king raised the great spear in his hand. Instantly eight thousand spears were lifted in answer, and from eight thousand throats came the royal cry of "Koom".

There was silence again, dead silence. Then the silence was broken. A soldier on our left dropped his shield.

Twala turned his cold eye in the direction of the noise.

"Come here," he said in a cruel voice.

A fine young man stepped out and stood in front of him.

"It was your shield that fell. Will you shame me in the eyes of these strangers from the stars? What have you to say?"

"It was by accident," he murmured.

"Then it is an accident for which you must pay. Scragga, let me see how you can use your spear. Kill this dog for me."

Scragga stepped forward. Once, twice he waved the spear, and then struck. The young soldier threw up his hands and dropped dead. From the crowd about us rose something like a murmur: it rolled round and round, and died away.

"It was a good stroke," said the king. "Take him away."

Four men carried away the body of the murdered man.

Sir Henry was boiling with anger. "Sit down!" I whispered.

Twala sat silent until the body had been removed. Then: "White people, where have you come from, and what do you want?"

"We come from the stars," I answered. "We have come to see this land."

"Remember that the stars are far off and you are near. Why should we not kill you?"

I laughed aloud – though there was no laughing in my heart.

"Haven't they told you how I strike with death from a distance?" I said.

"They have told me, but I do not believe them. Kill a man for me among those who stand over there."

"No," I answered. "We don't kill except to punish. But drive in a young elephant through the gates and I will strike it dead."

"Let it be done," he said.

"Now, Sir Henry," I said, "you must shoot. We want to show that I am not the only wizard of the party."

There was a pause. Then we saw an elephant coming through the gate. Seeing the great crowd of people, it stopped.

"Now!" I whispered.

Up went the gun. *Crack!* – and the beast was lying dead.

A whisper of wonder arose from the thousands around us.

Just then I saw the monkey-like figure creeping out from the shadow of the hut. When it reached the place where the king sat, I saw the face of a woman of great age, covered with deep yellow wrinkles. This was Gagool, the witch, so old that no one knew how old she was.

She laid her hand on the shoulder of Twala the king, and began to speak:

"Listen, King! Listen, soldiers! Listen, men and women! Listen. The spirit of life is in me, and I tell you the things that will be."

Terror seemed to seize the hearts of all who heard the words.

Gagool, Twala and Scragga

"Blood! Blood! Blood! Rivers of blood everywhere. I am old! I am old! Your fathers knew me, and their fathers' fathers. I have seen blood. Ha! Ha! But I will see more before I die.

"What do you want, White Men of the Stars? Have you come for white stones? You will find them when the blood is dry. But will you return to the place from which you came, or will you stop with me? Ha! Ha! Ha!

"And you with the dark proud face" – she pointed her finger at Umbopa – "who are you? I think I know. I think I can smell the smell of the blood in your heart. Take off that cloth——"

Her face suddenly became death-like, and she fell fainting to the ground.

The king rose up, shaking in every limb, and waved his hand. At once the soldiers began to march off, and in ten minutes, except for ourselves, the king and a few servants, the great space was left empty.

"White people," he said, "perhaps I should kill you. Gagool has spoken strange words."

I laughed. "Be careful, King. We are not easy to kill."

He put his hand to his forehead and thought.

"Go in peace," he said at last. "Tonight is a great dance. You must see it. Tomorrow I will think."

Chapter 9
The witches

On reaching our hut I asked Infadoos to enter with us.

"Infadoos," I said, "it seems to us that Twala the king is a cruel man."

"Yes, my lords. The land cries out because of his cruelty. Tonight you will see. The witches will smell out many and they will die. If the king wants to take a man's cattle or his wife, or if he fears a man, then Gagool, or some of the witches that she has taught, will smell that man out, and he will be killed. The land is weary of Twala and his red ways."

"Then why is it, Infadoos, that the people do not get rid of him?"

"If he were killed, Scragga would rule in his place, and the heart of Scragga is blacker than the heart of Twala his father. If Imotu had not been killed, or if Ignosi his son had lived, it might have been different; but they are both dead."

"No," said Umbopa.

"What do you mean, boy?" asked Infadoos.

"Listen, Infadoos," was the answer. "Years ago the king, Imotu, was killed in this country, and his wife ran away with the boy Ignosi. It was said that the woman and her son died on the mountains. But I tell you that the mother and the boy Ignosi did not die. They crossed the mountains and were led by some wandering desert-men across the sands beyond, till at last they came to water and grass and trees again."

"Surely you are mad to talk like that," said the old soldier.

"Do you think so? Look, I will show you, uncle."

Then with a single movement Umbopa slipped off the cloth that he wore and stood naked before us.

"Look," he said. And he pointed to the picture of a great creeping beast marked in his skin around his waist.

Infadoos looked with wide-open eyes. Then he fell on his knees.

"Koom! Koom!" he cried. "It is my brother's son; it is the king."

"Rise, Infadoos. I am not yet king; but, with your help, and with the help of these brave white men who are my friends, I will be. Yet the old witch Gagool was right: the land will run with blood first, and her blood must run with it, if she has any, for she killed my father with her words, and drove my mother away. Now, Infadoos, choose. Will you be my man?"

The old man went to where Umbopa (or rather, Ignosi) stood.

"Ignosi, true king of the Kukuanas, I am your man till death. When you were a babe, I played with you on my knees, and now my old arm will strike for you and freedom."

"And you, white men, will you help me?"

"Ignosi," I said, "you stood by us, and we will stand by you. But how do you intend to become king?"

"I do not know," replied Ignosi. "Infadoos, have you a plan?"

"Tonight," answered Infadoos, "the witches will work and there will be anger in the hearts of many against King Twala. When the dance is over, I will speak to some of the great chiefs and bring them here to show them that you are indeed the king. I think that by tomorrow you will have twenty thousand spears at your command."

Three men came to us, each carrying a shining shirt of chain armour and a fine battle-axe. They were gifts from the king.

When the full moon shone out, Infadoos arrived, in armour, with a guard of twenty men, to lead us to the dance. Infadoos asked us to put on the shirts of chain armour under our other clothes. They were rather large for Good and myself, but Sir Henry's fitted his splendid body perfectly. We took our pistols.

The great courtyard was filled by about twenty thousand men. Not a sound came from them.

"They are very silent," said Good.

"What does he say?" asked Infadoos.

I told him.

"Those that the shadow of Death is passing over are silent," he answered quietly.

"Tell me," I asked Infadoos, "are we in danger?"

"I don't know, my lords. I hope not. But you must not seem afraid. If you live through the night all may be well. The soldiers are murmuring against the king."

A small party came from the direction of the royal hut.

"It is the king, and Scragga his son, and Gagool; and with them are those who kill." Infadoos pointed to a little group of about a dozen gigantic men armed with spears.

"Look round, white lords," said Twala, and he rolled his one cruel eye from company to company. "See how they shake with fear, all those who have evil in their hearts and fear the judgement."

"Begin! begin!" cried Gagool, in her thin voice.

From out of the masses of soldiers, strange and terrible figures appeared running towards us. They were old women. Their white hair streamed out behind them as they ran. Their faces were painted with lines of white and yellow, and each held in her hand a bent stick. There were ten of them. They stopped in front of Gagool and cried: "Mother, Old Mother, we are here."

"Then go! The killers' spears are sharp. Go!"

Gagool's terrible pupils broke away in every direction. We could not watch them all, so we fixed our eyes on the witch who was nearest to us. When she came near the soldiers, she began to dance wildly, turning round and round, and crying, "I smell him, the evil-doer."

Quicker and quicker she danced till suddenly she stopped, and became still, like a dog smelling a rabbit. Then with a fierce cry she sprang in and touched a tall soldier with her bent stick. Instantly the two men standing next to him seized the unhappy man, one by each arm, and advanced with him towards the king. As he came, two of the killers stepped forward to meet him.

"Kill," said the king.

"Kill," cried Gagool.

Almost before the words were spoken, the terrible deed was done.

Another poor fellow was led up almost immediately after this. And so the game of death went on. Once we rose and tried to stop it, but Twala would not listen.

At last the witches seemed to tire of their bloody work, and we thought that it was all over. But it was not. To our surprise, Gagool rose from her place and moved forward. It was a strange sight to see this dreadful yellow-headed old creature slowly gather strength, until at last she rushed about almost as quickly as her terrible pupils. Suddenly she ran at a tall man standing in front of one of the companies, and touched him. As she did this, a deep cry went up from the company that he commanded. We

31

learnt afterwards that he was a man of great wealth and power, a cousin of the king.

Then Gagool began to draw nearer and nearer to us.

"Which is it to be?" Sir Henry asked himself.

In a moment she rushed in and touched Umbopa (Ignosi) on the shoulder.

"I smell him out," she cried. "Kill him! He is full of evil. Kill him, the stranger, before blood flows for him."

I stood up. "This man," I called, "is a servant of the king's guests. Whoever harms him harms us. By the law which binds guests and host, I claim protection for him."

"Gagool, mother of the witches, smelt him out: he must die," was the angry answer.

"He shall not die," I replied. "Whoever tries to touch him will himself die."

"Seize him!" roared Twala to the killers who stood around red with the blood of the dead.

"Stand back!" I shouted. "Stand back if you want to see tomorrow's light. If you touch him, your king dies," and I pointed my pistol at Twala. Sir Henry and Good also drew their pistols, Sir Henry pointing at the leading killer, and Good taking careful aim at Gagool.

Twala drew back as he saw the barrel of my pistol come in a line with his breast.

"Well," I said, "what is it to be, Twala?"

Then he spoke:

"You have claimed that he is my guest. For that reason, and not from fear of you, I spare him."

"I am glad," I answered quietly, "we are tired of death and want to sleep. Is the dance ended?"

"It is ended," said Twala in a low and angry voice.

He lifted his spear. The soldiers began to march away through the gateway in perfect silence.

Chapter 10
Before the battle

It was almost morning when Infadoos came to us, followed by half a dozen fine-looking chiefs.

"My lords and Ignosi, true king of the Kukuanas, I have brought with me these men, who are great men among us, each having command of three thousand soldiers. Now let them too see the mark of the Creeping Beast and hear your story, so that they may say whether they will join with you against Twala the king."

By way of answer Ignosi took off the cloth and showed the mark. Each chief in turn drew near and examined it by the dim light of the lamp.

Then Ignosi put on his cloth again, and repeated the story which he had told us in the morning.

Infadoos said, "Will you stand by this man and help him to be king as his father was, or will you not? The land cries out against Twala, and the people's blood flows like water. You have seen tonight."

The chiefs moved to one side and spoke in low voices. Then Infadoos came back to us.

"Three kilometres from Loo," he said, "there is a hill shaped like a half-moon. There my soldiers, and three other companies that these chiefs command, are waiting. We will make a plan so that two or three other companies may be moved there too. Tonight I will take you and lead you out of Loo to that place. There you will be safe. And from there we can make war on Twala the king."

Very late that night, we reached the hill where Infadoos and six chiefs had put their men.

Chapter 11
The battle

At sunrise we made ourselves ready. Sir Henry put on chain armour under his clothes, and a very fine sight he was. He carried a great battle-axe.

We went out and found Infadoos with his own men, the Greys, the finest set of men in the Kukuana army. Ignosi joined us. The men were watching the army of Twala beginning to march out of Loo in a long line.

Infadoos and Ignosi spoke to the soldiers. They gave the royal greeting of "Koom", which was a sign that they accepted Ignosi as their king.

"Infadoos, my uncle," said Ignosi, "You see how the hill bends round like a half-moon and how the plain runs like a green tongue towards us inside it. Let your company, my uncle, advance with one other company down to the green tongue. When Twala sees it, he will throw his whole army against it to destroy it. But the place is narrow, and the companies can only come against you one at a time. While the eyes of all Twala's army are fixed on the fight on the narrow tongue, the rest of our army will creep along the two horns of the hill, and will attack Twala's army from the two sides."

The arrangements for the battle were made very rapidly, for the soldiers were well drilled. The men hastily took a meal and then marched off to their places.

Then Good came up to Sir Henry and myself.

"Goodbye, you fellows," he said, "I am off to the people on the right. I have come to shake hands in case we don't meet again." We shook hands in silence.

"It's a strange business," said Sir Henry, "but I don't

expect to see tomorrow's sun. I'll be with the Greys. The Greys will have to fight until there isn't a man left of them so as to let the rest of the army get round the sides. Well, it will be a man's death. Goodbye, old fellow."

In another moment, Good had gone. Infadoos came up and led Sir Henry to his place in the front line of the Greys. I went with Ignosi to my place with the second company, who were behind, supporting the Greys.

By the time we reached the edge of the slope, the Greys were already half-way down. Twala's army had now drawn near. They had observed the movement of the Greys, and company after company was starting forward, hurrying to reach the root of the tongue of land before the Greys could come out on to the plain. The Greys reached the centre of the tongue, where it became broader. There they stopped.

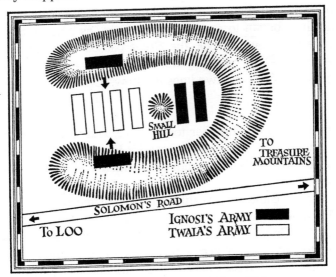

Plan of the Battle of Half-Moon Hill

We moved down and took our place about a hundred metres behind them on slightly higher ground.

Twala's army began to enter the valley. They discovered that the space was so narrow that only one company could advance at a time, and in front of them they saw the famous Greys, the glory of the Kukuana army. They paused. There was no eagerness to attack those three lines of fierce fighters who stood so firm and so ready. Then I saw Twala himself. He gave an order, and the first company of the enemy, raising a shout, charged up towards the Greys.

The Greys remained perfectly still and silent until the attackers were within forty metres. Then suddenly with a roar they sprang forward with uplifted spears; and the two lines met. The sound of the meeting shields came to our ears like thunder. The mass of struggling men swung this way and that, but not for long. Suddenly the attacking lines began to grow thinner. Then, as when a great wave flows over a rock, the Greys passed over them. It was done. That company was completely destroyed. But the Greys had only two lines left now. One third of them were dead.

They closed up shoulder to shoulder, and waited for the second attack. I was glad to see Sir Henry's yellow beard as he moved about arranging the men. So he was still alive!

Again came the dreadful thunder of meeting shields. This time the struggle was longer. Just when we thought that the Greys were defeated, and when we were preparing to take their place, I heard Sir Henry's deep voice ringing out, and saw his circling battle-axe as he waved it high above his head. Then came a change. The Greys

Sir Henry and the Greys in battle

stood still as a rock against which the waves of spearmen broke again and again. Then they began to move once more – forward this time. The attackers broke away in flying groups, their white head-dresses streaming in the wind.

Of the Greys, less than a quarter remained. And yet they shouted and waved their spears. Then, instead of falling back, as we expected, they ran forward after the flying groups of men to a little piece of rising ground, and formed three rings around it. There I saw Sir Henry, unhurt, with our old friend Infadoos. Then Twala's companies rolled down upon them, and once more the battle closed in.

"Are we to stand here till we put out roots, Ignosi, while Twala swallows our brothers there?" I asked.

As I spoke, a company of the enemy rushed past the ring on the small hill and attacked it from the nearer side.

"Now is the moment," cried Ignosi. Lifting his battle-axe he gave the sign to advance, and we charged with a rush like the rush of the sea.

What followed, it is out of my power to describe. There was a terrible shock, a roar of voices, and a flashing of spears seen through a red mist of blood. When my mind cleared, I found myself inside the ring of the Greys just behind Sir Henry himself.

Again and again they attacked us, and again and again we beat them back. But every moment our circle grew smaller. It was a fine sight to see that old soldier, Infadoos, as calm as ever, giving orders, laughing from time to time just to keep up the spirits of his few remaining men; then, as each charge rolled on, stepping forward to wherever the fighting was thickest, to take his share.

Even finer was the sight of Sir Henry. None could live where he struck.

Just as that instant there rose a cry of despair from the soldiers who were attacking us. To the right and left the plain was alive with charging men. Our men had worked round the sides and were attacking the enemy from all directions at once. The moment could not have been better chosen. Just as Ignosi had expected, all Twala's army had fixed their eyes on the bloody struggle which was going on round the Greys. It was not until our horns were closing upon them that they dreamt of our approach. And now, before they could get their men into proper order to defend themselves, our attackers had leapt on their sides.

In five minutes the fate of the battle was decided. Twala's companies broke and fled. Soon the whole plain between us and Loo was scattered with groups of running men, flying from the battle-ground. As for the men who had been attacking our circle, they melted away as though by magic, and we were left standing there like a rock from which the sea has retired. But what a sight it was! Around us the dead and dying lay in masses. Of the brave Greys there remained only ninety-five men on their feet. More than three thousand four hundred had fallen, most of them never to rise again.

We marched to Loo.

On arriving at the nearest gate, we found a company of our men watching it. The officer in command of these men greeted Ingosi as king, and told him that Twala's army was inside the town, and that Twala himself was there too. He said that they were thoroughly beaten and would probably not try to stop us. Ignosi sent forward a man to the gate, ordering the defenders to open it, and promising, on his royal word, life and forgiveness to every man who laid down his arms. Soon after this, the gate was opened, and we marched into the town.

All along the road stood soldiers, with bent heads, their shields and spears at their feet. As Ignosi passed, they greeted him as king. We marched straight to Twala's hut. We found the great space deserted. No, not quite deserted, for there, on the farther side in front of his hut, sat Twala. Only one person was with him – Gagool.

It was a sad sight to see him, his battle-axe and shield by his side, his head bent, with just one old woman with him.

Our party advanced towards him, Gagool cursing us as we came. At last Twala lifted his head; his one eye seemed to flash almost as brightly as the great diamond bound round his forehead, as he fixed his gaze on Ignosi.

"Greeting, King," he said in cold anger. "What fate have you for me?"

"The fate which you gave to my father," was the answer.

"It is good. But I demand the right of the Kukuana royal house – to die fighting."

Infadoos had told us that it is a law of the Kukuanas that a man of royal blood may not be put to death. He is allowed to choose one man after another to fight him until one of them kills him.

"You have the right," said Ignosi. "Choose. Who will you fight with? Myself, I cannot fight with you, for a king fights only in war."

Twala's eye ran up and down our line, and I felt for a moment that it rested on me. What if he chose to begin by fighting me? What chance should I have against that huge man, nearly two metres tall?

Then Twala spoke, turning to Sir Henry:

"What do you say? Or are you afraid?"

"No," said Ignosi hastily. "You shall not fight with him."

"Not if he is afraid," said Twala.

Unfortunately Sir Henry understood these words, and the blood flamed up into his cheeks.

"I will fight him," he said. "No living man shall call me afraid. I am ready now," and he stepped forward and lifted his axe.

Twala laughed, and, stepping forward, faced Sir Henry.

Then they began to circle round each other, their battle-axes raised.

Suddenly Sir Henry sprang forward and struck a fearful blow at Twala, who stepped to one side. So heavy was the stroke that the striker nearly fell forward after it. Twala was quick to seize his chance. Swinging his great battle-axe round his head, he brought it down with terrible force. But with a quick movement of the left arm Sir Henry set his shield between himself and the blow. The edge of the shield was cut away and the blow fell on his left shoulder, but not heavily enough to do any serious damage. In another moment Sir Henry got in a second blow which was also received by Twala upon his shield. Then followed blow upon blow. The excited onlookers shouted at every stroke.

Sir Henry caught a fresh stroke on his shield and then hit out with all his force. The blow cut through Twala's shield and through the chain-armour behind it, wounding him in the shoulder. With a cry of pain Twala returned

41

the blow, and such was his strength that he cut through the handle of Sir Henry's battle-axe and wounded him in the face.

A cry of despair rose from the onlookers as the head of Sir Henry's axe fell to the ground. Twala again raised his axe and rushed at him with a shout.

The next moment I saw Sir Henry's shield lying on the ground and Sir Henry himself with his great arms round Twala's waist. This way and that they swung, using all their strength. Twala swung Sir Henry right off his feet; and down they came together, rolling over and over on the ground, Twala striking out at Sir Henry's head with the battle-axe, and Sir Henry trying to drive his knife through Twala's armour.

It was a fierce struggle, and a terrible thing to see.

"Get his axe," shouted Good; and perhaps Sir Henry heard him. He dropped the knife and reached out at the axe which was fastened to Twala's arm by a piece of leather. Still rolling over and over, they fought for it like wild cats. Suddenly the leather string burst. Sir Henry got free, the weapon remaining in his hand. At once he was on his feet, the red blood streaming from the wound in his face, and so was Twala. Drawing his heavy knife he rushed straight at Sir Henry and struck him on the breast; but the chain armour stood against the blow. Again he struck, and again the knife leapt back. Then, swinging the big axe round his head, Sir Henry hit at him with all his force. There was a shout of excitement from a thousand throats. Twala's head seemed to spring from his shoulders. Sir Henry, faint from loss of blood, fell heavily across the body of the dead king.

Chapter 12
The Place of Death

Sir Henry soon recovered his strength. Meanwhile, Igno-si held a great meeting and was recognised as king by all the chiefs. The remaining men of the Greys were thanked before the whole army for their splendid fighting in the great battle. The king gave each man a large present of cattle, and he made them officers in the new company of Greys which was being formed.

Afterwards we had a short visit from Ignosi, on whose forehead the royal diamond was now bound.

"Greeting, King," I said, rising.

"Yes, king at last, with the help of you three great men," he answered.

I asked him what he had decided to do with Gagool.

"I ought to kill her," he answered, "and all the other witches with her. She has lived so long that no one can remember when she was not old. She has always trained the witches and made the land evil."

"But she knows a lot," I said. "It is easier to destroy knowledge than to gather it."

"That is true," he said. "She alone knows the secret of the Silent Ones over there where the great road runs. But I have discovered something. There is a great cave deep in the mountain where the dead kings of the land are put: it is their grave. There you will find Twala's body, sitting with those who went before him. There also is a deep hole from which at some time long ago men got the precious stones. There, too, in the Place of Death, is a secret room known only to Gagool. Yet there is a story in the land that many, many years ago a white man crossed

43

the mountains and was led by a woman to the secret room and was shown the wealth hidden in it. But before he could take it, the woman told the king about him, and he was driven back to the mountains."

"The story is true, Ignosi. We found the white man," I said.

"Yes, we found him," answered Ignosi. "And now, if you can reach that secret room, and the stones are there, you may have as many of them as you can take – if indeed you wish to leave me, my brothers."

"First we must find the secret room," I said.

"There is only one person who can show it to you – Gagool," replied Ignosi.

"And if she will not?"

"Then she must die," answered Ignosi. "I have saved her alive only for this." He called a man and ordered Gagool to be brought to him.

In a few minutes she came, hurried along by two guards who she was cursing as she walked.

"Leave her," said the king. She sank on to the floor.

"What do you want of me, Ignosi?" she said. "If you touch me, I will kill you with my magic."

"Your magic could not save Twala, and it cannot hurt me," was the answer. "Listen. You must tell me the way to the secret room where the shining stones are hidden."

"Ha! Ha!" she cried, "Nobody else knows its secret, and I will never tell you."

Slowly Ignosi brought his spear down.

With a cry Gagool rolled on the floor.

"I will show it. Only let me live and sit in the sun, and I will show you."

"Very well. Tomorrow you shall go with Infadoos, and

44

my white brothers, and be careful that you do not fail, or you will die – slowly."

"I will not fail, Ignosi. I always keep my promise. Once before a woman showed the secret room to a white man, and evil came to him." Her eyes shone. "Her name was Gagool too. Perhaps I was that woman."

"You lie," I said. "That was hundreds of years ago."

"Perhaps. Perhaps it was my mother's mother who told me. Her name was Gagool. You will find in the place a bag full of stones. The man filled the bag, but he never took it away. Evil came to him."

The party contained our three selves, Infadoos and Gagool. She was carried, and, under the covering which hid her, she could be heard murmuring and cursing.

We marched along Solomon's great road to the foot of the centre hill, and there stopped. For an hour and a half we climbed up a path.

At last we saw before us a huge hole in the ground, a hundred metres deep.

"What's this?" Sir Henry wanted to know.

"You may be sure that this is Solomon's diamond mine," I said.

We went on, eager to see the three towering objects that we had seen on the other side of the mine. As we drew near, we saw that they were huge human figures, cut out of the rock. These were the "Silent Ones".

Straight in front of us rose a wall of rock about twenty-five metres high. Gagool carried a lamp in her hand. She gave us one evil look, then, leaning on a stick, moved off towards this wall. We followed her till we came to a narrow arched door.

"Now, white men from the stars," she said, "are you ready? I am here to obey the orders of my lord the king, and to show you the store of bright stones."

"We are ready," I said.

"Good! Good! Make strong your hearts to bear what you shall see. Are you coming too, Infadoos?"

"No," replied Infadoos, "it is not right for me to enter there. But be careful how you deal with my lords. If a hair of them is hurt, Gagool, you die. Do you hear?"

"I hear. I will obey the orders of the king. I have obeyed the orders of many kings, till in the end they obeyed mine. Ha! Ha! I am going to look at their faces once more – and Twala's. Come on, come on, here is the lamp."

Gagool passed through the door. The way was narrow, just wide enough for two to go side by side. When we had gone about fifty metres we saw that the way was growing faintly light. Another minute and we were in perhaps the most wonderful place that anyone has ever seen.

Think of the hugest hall you ever stood in, without windows, but dimly lighted from above, and you will get some idea of the great cave in which we found ourselves.

Running in rows down its sides were gigantic towers of what looked like ice, but they had really been formed by the action of the drops of water falling from the roof. Each drop carries in it certain salts, which in time become as hard as ice. In this way, in hundreds of years, the falling drops had built up towers of glassy material. High above, hanging from the roof, the points of huge icy needles could dimly be seen.

We could hear the way these things were built. Every few moments, with a tiny sound, a drop of water fell from

46

The huge cave

the far-off needle onto the tower below. In about a thousand years the tower would be raised thirty centimetres.

Gagool led us straight to the end of the great silent cave, where we found another doorway.

"Are you prepared to enter the Place of Death, white men?" asked Gagool, in the hope of making us uncomfortable.

"Lead on," said Good, trying to look as if he was not at all alarmed.

After about twenty steps we found ourselves in a room about twelve metres long and ten metres broad which had been cut out of the mountain by hand-labour. It was not so well lit as the great cave, and at first all I could see was a stone table running down the whole length of it, with a huge white figure at its head and white figures seated all round it. There was a brown thing on the table in the centre. In another moment my eyes became accustomed to the light, and I saw what these things were.

It was a terrible sight. There at the end of the table, holding in his bony fingers a great white spear, sat Death himself. The figure was shaped in the form of a huge human body, five metres high. This must be the White Death in José da Silvestre's letter.

"What are those things?" asked Good, pointing to the white company round the table.

"Hee! Hee! Hee!" laughed Gagool. "To those who enter the Hall of the Dead, evil comes. Hee! Hee! Come, you who are so brave in battle, come and see the man you killed." And the old creature caught Sir Henry's coat in her skinny fingers and led him away towards the table. We followed.

Then she stopped and pointed at the brown object on the table. There, quite naked, seated on the table was the body of Twala, last king of the Kukuanas, with its head on its knees – the head that Sir Henry had cut off in the fight. Over the body was gathered a thin glassy covering which made it appear even more terrible. At first we could not understand this. Then we observed that from the roof the water fell steadily drop by drop on to the neck and ran down over the dead body. Then I guessed what this glassy covering was. Twala's body was being changed by just the same action as had made those wonderful towers and needles in the great cave. Twala's body was being changed into stone!

I looked at the white forms round the stone table. They were human bodies – or rather they had been human; now they had become stone. This was the way in which the Kukuana people had from ancient times preserved their royal dead. Exactly how it was done, I never discovered – whether they merely placed them for a number of years under the falling drop, or whether something else was done; but there they sat, iced over, and preserved for ever.

Chapter 13
Solomon's Treasure House

"Now, Gagool," I said in a low voice, for somehow one dared not speak above a whisper in that place, "lead us to the treasure room."

"My lords are not afraid?" she said, looking up into my face.

"Lead on."

"Very good, my lords." She went round to the back of great Death. "Here is the room."

She put the lamp she had been carrying on the floor, and leaned herself against the side of the cave. I took a match and lit the lamp, and then looked for the doorway; but there was nothing before us except the wall of rock.

Gagool laughed. "The way is there, my lords. Ha! Ha!"

"I do not see it," I answered angrily.

"Look!" and she pointed at the rock.

As she did so, we saw that a mass of stone was rising slowly from the floor and disappearing into the rock above. Very slowly and gently the great stone raised itself, until at last a dark hole was seen in the place where it had been.

Our excitement was great when we saw the way to Solomon's Treasure House thrown open at last. Would it prove to be nothing after all, I wondered, or was old da Silvestre right? Was there huge wealth stored in that dark place, wealth which would make us the richest men in the whole world? We should know in a minute or two.

"Enter, white men from the stars," said Gagool, advancing into the doorway, "but first listen to Gagool the old. The bright stones that you will see were taken from the hole over which the Silent Ones sit, and were stored here by someone – I don't know who. Only once has this place been entered since the time when those who stored the stones departed, leaving them behind. It happened that a white man reached this country from over the mountains and was well received by the king of that day – that king who sits there," and she pointed to the fifth king at the Table of the Dead. "There was a woman of this country who by a chance had learnt the secret of the door: you might search for a thousand years and you would never find it. The white man entered with this woman. He found the stones, and filled the skin of a small goat with them. As he was going, he took up one more stone, a large one, and held it in his hand." Here she paused.

"Well," I asked, "what happened to da Silvestre?"

The old creature seemed surprised at hearing his name.

"How do you know the dead man's name?" she asked quickly. Then, without waiting for an answer, she went on: "For some reason the white man became frightened, for he threw down the goat-skin, and ran out with only the one stone in his hand. And that stone the king took, and it is the stone which was taken from Twala's forehead, the stone which Ignosi now wears."

"Has nobody entered here since?" I asked, trying to see into the dark room.

"Nobody, my lords. Every king has opened it, but he has not entered. There is a saying that those who enter will die within one month, just as the white man died in the cave on the mountain where you found him. Ha! Ha! Mine are true words."

How did the old creature know all these things?

"Enter, my lords. If I speak truth, the goat-skin with the stones will lie on the floor; and whether it is true that it is death to enter – that you will learn afterwards. Ha! Ha! Ha!"

She passed through the doorway, taking the lamp with her. We followed.

About fifteen metres beyond the entrance, we came suddenly to a curiously painted wooden door. It was standing open. Whoever was last there had not found the time, or had forgotten, to shut it.

Just in this doorway lay a bag, formed of goat-skin, that appeared to be full of stones.

"Hee! Hee!" laughed Gagool, as the light from her lamp fell upon it. "Did I not tell you that the white man who came here left hastily and dropped the bag? That is it!"

Good bent down and lifted it.

"By heaven! I believe it's full of diamonds," he said in a whisper.

"Go on," said Sir Henry. "Here, give me the lamp." He took it from Gagool's hand and stepped through the doorway.

We followed, forgetting for the moment the bag of diamonds, and found ourselves in Solomon's Treasure Room.

It was a room cut out of the rock, and not more than three metres square.

"My lords, look over there where it is darkest, if you want to find the stones," said Gagool. "There are three stone chests, two shut and one open."

"Look in that corner, Sir Henry," I said.

"Great heavens!" he cried. "Look here."

We hurried across to where he was standing. There were three stone chests up against the wall.

Sir Henry held the lamp over the open chest.

The chest was three-quarters full of uncut diamonds, most of them of large size.

We stood still and gazed, the lamp in the middle and the glimmering jewels below.

"Hee! hee! hee!" laughed old Gagool behind us. "There are the bright stones you love, as many as you like. Take them in your fingers. *Eat* them, hee! hee! *Drink* them, ha! ha!"

There they were, millions of pounds' worth of diamonds, only waiting to be taken away.

We set to work to open the other two chests. The first of them was full to the top. The other was only about a quarter full, but the stones were chosen ones, some as large as eggs.

What we did not see was the look of fearful hatred on old Gagool's face as she crept out of the treasure-room towards the great door of rock.

Suddenly I realised what was happening. "Come on!" I cried.

We started running; and this is what the light from the lamp showed us. The door of rock was closing down slowly; it was less than a metre from the floor.

Gagool threw herself on the ground to creep under the closing stone. She was under – ah! No! She had forgotten that she was too old to move quickly through a narrow gap. The stone caught her. She shouted in terrible pain. Down, down it came, all the huge weight of it. Cry after cry such as we had never heard! Then a long dreadful *crack,* and the door was shut, just as, rushing down, we threw ourselves against it.

It was all done in a few moments.

"She's dead!" cried Good. "What a terrible death!"

"You needn't let that trouble you, old fellow," said Sir Henry.

"Eh!" said Good. "What do you mean?"

"I mean that we will soon join her. Don't you see that the door is shut, and that this is our grave."

For a few minutes we stood there. All the strength seemed to have gone out of us. The first shock of this idea of the slow and terrible end that we must expect silenced us. We saw it now: that she-devil Gagool had planned this for us from the first. It must have been just the kind of idea that her evil mind would have enjoyed, the idea of the three men slowly dying of thirst and hunger in the company of the treasure they had desired. Now I saw the meaning of her words about "eating" and "drinking" the diamonds. Perhaps someone had tried to treat poor old da Silvestre in the same way when he dropped the skin full of jewels.

"We must do something," said Sir Henry. "The lamp will soon go out. Let's see if we can find the handle that works the rock."

We sprang forward and began to feel up and down the door and the rock at the sides. But we could discover nothing.

"You can be sure," I said, "that it can't be opened from the inside. If it could, Gagool wouldn't have risked trying to creep underneath the stone."

"We can do nothing with the door," said Sir Henry. "Let's go back to the treasure room."

The chests of diamonds

We sat down with our backs against the three stone chests of diamonds.

We had brought a basket of food and some water with us. There was enough food and water to support life for about two days.

We each ate a little and drank some water.

We did not feel hungry though we were really in great need of food. We felt better after swallowing it. Then we got up and began to examine the walls and floor of our prison in the faint hope of finding some way out.

There was none. It was unlikely that there would be any second entrance to a treasure room.

"Quatermain," said Sir Henry, "what is the time?"

I looked to see. It was six o'clock. We had entered the cave at eleven.

"Infadoos will miss us," I said. "If we don't return tonight, he will search for us in the morning."

"He doesn't know the secret of the door," replied Sir Henry, "nor even where it is. Even if he found the door he couldn't break it down. All the Kukuana army couldn't break through more than a metre of rock."

The lamp grew dimmer.

Then it burned bright for a moment and showed the whole scene, the goat-skin full of treasure, the dim glimmer of the diamonds, and the white faces of us three men seated there waiting for death.

Then the flame sank down, and went out.

Chapter 14
We lose hope

I can't give any real description of the night that followed.
We were fortunate to sleep a little, but I myself found it
impossible to sleep much. It was not so much the thought
of the terrible death drawing so near, as the *silence* which
prevented me from sleeping. We all know what it is to lie
awake at night, and feel the silence press on us, but most
of us have no idea what perfect silence is. In a house
there is always some sound that, though we may not hear
it, takes off the sharp edge of perfect silence. But here
there was none. We were prisoners in the centre of a
huge snow-topped mountain. Thousands of metres above
us the fresh air rushed over the white snow, but no sound
of it reached us. More than a metre of rock separated us
from even the dreadful Hall of the Dead; and the dead
make no noise. All the guns of earth and the thunder of
heaven could not have come to our ears. We were cut off
from every murmur of the world.

And there around us lay treasures enough for a whole
nation, yet we would have given them all gladly for the
faintest chance of escape. Soon, no doubt, we would wish
we could change them for a bit of food or a cup of water,
and after that even for the mercy of a speedy end to our
sufferings.

"Good," said Sir Henry's voice at last, and it sounded
terrible in that great stillness, "how many matches have
you got in the box?"

"Eight."

"Strike one and let's see the time."

He did so, and, after that black darkness, the flame nearly blinded us. It was five o'clock. The beautiful dawn was now glowing rose-red on the snow far over our heads, and the wind would be awakening the night mists in the hollows.

"We had better eat something and keep up our strength," I said.

"What is the use of eating?" answered Good. "The sooner we die and get it over, the better."

"While there is life, there is hope," said Sir Henry.

So we ate, and then drank a little water.

Time passed.

Then we got as near to the door as possible and shouted on the faint chance of somebody catching a sound outside. Good, from long practice at sea, made a fearful noise. I never heard such shouts. They produced no effect.

After a time we gave it up and came back, very thirsty. Then we stopped shouting, as it used up our supply of water too quickly.

So we sat down once more against the chests of useless diamonds. There was nothing to do, and we could do nothing.

Ah, how good and how brave Sir Henry Curtis was! Forgetting his own share of troubles he did all he could to cheer us, telling stories of men who had made wonderful escapes when all hope had been lost. And, when these failed to cheer us, he pointed out that the end, which must come to us all, would be very soon over, and that such a death would be a very easy one (which was not true).

His was a beautiful character, very quiet and very strong.

And so somehow the day went on as the night had gone – if, indeed, one can use these words when all was the blackest night. When we lit a match to see the time, it was seven o'clock.

Once more we ate and drank, and, as we did so, an idea came to me.

"How is it," I said, "that the air in this place keeps fresh?"

"Great heavens!" said Good, "I never thought of that! It can't come through the stone door: that would let no air through. It must come from somewhere. If there was no air coming in, we should not be able to breathe by now. Let's have a look."

It was wonderful what a change this mere glimmer of hope made in us. In a moment we were all creeping about on our hands and knees, feeling, feeling for the slightest sign of incoming air. For an hour or more we went on, till at last Sir Henry and I gave it up in despair. But Good still continued, saying, with some cheerfulness, that it was better than doing nothing.

"I say, you fellows," he said, after some time, in an excited voice, "come here."

I need not tell you that we went towards the sound of his voice quickly enough.

"Quatermain, put your hand here, where mine is. Now do you feel anything?"

"I think I feel air coming up."

"Now listen." He rose and struck the place with his heel: a flame of hope shot up in our hearts; it rang hollow.

With shaking hands I lit a match. There were only three matches left. As the match burnt, we examined the spot. There was a crack in the rock-floor, and – great heavens! – set level with the rock, there was a stone ring.

We said no word; we were too excited to speak. Good
had a knife. He opened it and worked round the ring to
loosen it. Finally he worked it under the ring and pressed
it gently up. The ring began to move. Soon he had got
the ring up. He put his hands into it and pulled with all
his force; but nothing moved.

"Let me try," I said. I took hold and pulled, but with
no result.

Then Sir Henry tried, and failed.

Good worked his knife all round the crack where we
felt the air coming up. Then he took off a strong black silk
handkerchief which he wore, and passed it through the
ring. "Quatermain, take Sir Henry round the middle and
pull when I give the word. Now!"

Sir Henry put out all his huge strength, and Good and
I did the same with such power as Nature had given us.

"Pull! Pull! It's moving!" said Sir Henry. Suddenly
there was a cracking sound, then a rush of air, and we
were all on our backs on the floor, with a heavy stone on
the top of us. Sir Henry's strength had done it; never did
strength help a man more.

"Light a match, Quatermain," he said, as soon as we
had got up and recovered our breath. "Carefully now."

I did so, and there before us, heaven be praised! was
the first step of a set of stone stairs.

"Now what is to be done?" asked Good.

"Follow the stairs, of course, and trust to our good
fortune."

"Stop!" said Sir Henry. "Quatermain, get the meat
and the water that are left. We may need them."

I went back to our place by the chests. As I was coming
away, an idea struck me. I thought I might put a few of

the diamonds in my pocket in the hope that we might get out of this terrible place. So I put my hand into the first chest and filled the pockets of my coat, and finally I put in a few of the big ones from the third chest.

"I say, you fellows," I said, "won't you take some diamonds with you? I've filled my pockets,"

"Oh, curse the diamonds," said Sir Henry. "I hope I never see another one."

As for Good, he made no answer.

"Come on, Quatermain," said Sir Henry, who was already standing on the first step of the stone stairs. "Steady, I will go first."

"Be careful where you put your feet," I answered. "There may be some hole underneath."

"More probably another room," said Sir Henry.

He descended slowly, counting the steps as he went. When he got to fifteen he stopped. "This is the bottom," he said. "Thank heaven there seems to be a sort of way on. Come on down."

On reaching the bottom we lit one of the two remaining matches. By its light we saw two narrow doorways, left and right, in front of us. There arose the question of which way to go. Then Good remembered that when I lit the match the air blew the flame to the left. "Let us go against the wind," he said. "Air blows inwards not outwards." So we went to the right against the wind.

Feeling along the wall with one hand and trying the ground before us at every step, we departed from that cursed treasure room on our terrible search for life.

We went on for about quarter of an hour. Then the path took a sharp turn, or else ran into another path. We followed this, and in time we were led into a third path. And so it went on for some hours.

At last we stopped, thoroughly weary, and almost in despair again. We seemed to be lost in these endless underground ways. We ate our last piece of meat and drank our last drop of water. It seemed that we had escaped death in the dreadful darkness of the treasure room only to meet it in the darkness of these underground ways.

Then I thought that I caught a sound. I told the others to listen too. It was very faint and very far off; but it was a sound, a faint, murmuring sound. The others heard it too, and no words can describe the blessedness of it after all those hours of utter stillness.

"By heaven! It's running water," said Good. "Come on."

Off we started again in the direction from which the faint murmur seemed to come, feeling our way as before, along the rocky walls. As we went, the sound became clearer, till at last it seemed quite loud in the quiet of the place. On and on: now we could hear the rush of the water quite plainly. Now we were quite near to it, and Good, who was leading, said that he could smell it.

"Go gently, Good," said Sir Henry. "We must be close."

Suddenly there came a cry from Good. He had fallen in.

"Good! Good!" we shouted in terror, "where are you?" Then, to our joy, an answer came back in a faint voice.

"I've got hold of a rock. Strike a light to show me where you are."

Hastily I hit the last remaining match. Its faint light showed us a dark mass of water running at our feet, and some way out was the dim form of our companion holding on to a rock.

"Be ready to catch me," shouted Good. "I'll have to swim."

We heard a struggling in the water. In another minute he had caught Sir Henry's hand and we had pulled him up out of the water.

"My word!" he said. "That was a near escape. The stream is terribly fast. If I hadn't caught that rock, I should have been finished."

We dared not follow the river in case we fell into it again in the darkness. We had a good drink of the water, and then went back the way we had come.

At last we came to a path leading to our right. "We may as well take it," said Sir Henry. "All roads are the same here. We can only go on until we drop."

Utterly tired out, we struggled along, Sir Henry now leading the way.

Suddenly he stopped, and we fell against his back.

"Look!" he whispered. "Am I going mad? Or is that light?"

We gazed, and there, yes, there far away in front of us was a faint glimmering spot.

With a cry of hope we went on. In five minutes there was no longer any doubt, it was a glimmer of light. A minute more and a breath of real live air came to us. The way became narrower. Sir Henry went on his knees. The way became smaller and smaller. It was earth now: the rock had ended.

A struggle, and Sir Henry was out; and so was Good; and so was I. And there above us were the blessed stars, and the sweet air was on our faces. Then suddenly something gave way, and we were all rolling over and over through grass and bushes and soft wet soil.

I caught at something and stopped. A shout came from Sir Henry who had been stopped by some level ground. We found Good caught by the root of a tree.

We sat down together there on the grass. I think we cried for joy. We had escaped from that terrible room that was so near to becoming our grave. And see, there on the mountain was the dawn that we had never hoped to see again.

The grey light of day came creeping down the slopes, and we saw that we were at the bottom, or nearly at the bottom, of the deep mine in front of the entrance of the cave.

The day grew brighter. We could see each other now. Hollow-cheeked, hollow-eyed, covered with dust and dirt and blood, the long fear of death still written on our faces, we were a terrible sight.

We rose, and with slow and painful movements, began to struggle up the sloping sides.

At last it was done. We stood by the great road. At the side of the road, a hundred metres away, a fire was burning, and round the fire were men. We moved towards them, supporting one another and stopping after every few steps. Then one of the men rose, saw us, and fell on the ground crying out for fear.

"Infadoos, Infadoos! It is your friends."

He rose and ran towards us. "Oh, my lords, my lords, back from the dead!"

Chapter 15
Found!

Ten days later we were back in our huts in Loo, surprisingly not greatly harmed by our terrible experience.

Ignosi listened with the greatest interest to our wonderful story. When we told him of Gagool's end, he became thoughtful. "That was a strange woman," he said. "I am glad that she is dead."

"And now, Ignosi," I said, "the time has come for us to say goodbye. You came with us as a servant, and we leave you as a great king. May you rule justly, and may success go with you. Tomorrow at sunrise will you give us some men who will lead us across the mountains?"

Ignosi covered his face with his hands. Then at last he answered: "My heart is heavy. What have I done to cause you to leave me? You who stood by me in battle, will you leave me in the day of peace and victory?"

I laid my hand on his arm. "Ignosi," I said, "when you wandered in Zululand, didn't your heart turn to the land your mother told you of, your native land, where first you saw the light, where you played when you were little, the land where your place was?"

"That is true."

"In the same way, Ignosi, our hearts turn to our land and to our own place."

There was a silence. When Ignosi broke it, it was in a different voice.

"Infadoos, my uncle, will guide you. Goodbye, my brothers. Go now, in case my eyes rain down tears like a woman's. At times, as you look back down the path of life, or when you are old and gather yourselves together to sit by the fire because for you the sun has no more heat, you will think how we stood shoulder to shoulder in the great battle. Goodbye for ever, my lords and friends."

Ignosi rose and gazed at us for a few moments. Then he threw the corner of his garment over his head so as to cover his face from us.

We went in silence.

As we travelled, Infadoos told us that there was another way over the mountains. He also told us that, a few days' march from the mountains on that side, there was a sort of island of trees and rich land in the middle of the desert. We had always wondered how Ignosi's mother with the child lived through the dangers of that long journey across the mountains and the desert. It was now clear to us that she must have taken this second path.

At last we had to say goodbye to that true friend and fine old soldier, Infadoos. He solemnly wished all good upon us, and nearly wept with grief. After seeing that our guides had plenty of water and food, we shook him by the hand. His soldiers gave a thundering farewell cry of "Koom"; and we began our downward climb.

By noon of the third day's journey from the foot of the mountains, we could see the trees Infadoos had spoken of, and within an hour of sunset we were walking once more on grass and listening to the sound of running water ...

And now I come to perhaps the strangest thing that happened to us in all this strange adventure.

I was walking along quietly some way in front of the other two, when suddenly I stopped. There, not twenty metres in front of me, was a pretty little hut.

The door of the hut opened, and there came out of it a

white man dressed in skins. He seemed to be walking painfully as if his right leg were broken. He had a large black beard. I thought that I must have gone mad. It was impossible. No hunter ever came to such a place as this. Certainly no hunter would ever settle in it. I stood gazing at the other man, and he stood and gazed at me. Just at this moment Sir Henry and Good walked up.

Sir Henry looked, and Good looked, and then all of a sudden the white man with the black beard uttered a great cry and began to come towards us. When he was close, he fell down in a sort of faint.

With a spring Sir Henry was by his side.

"Great heavens," he cried, "it's my brother, George!"

Hearing the sound, another figure also clothed in skins, came from the hut, a gun in his hand, and ran towards us. On seeing me, he too gave a cry.

"Don't you know me?" he shouted. "I'm Jim the hunter. We have been here nearly two years." And he fell at my feet, weeping for joy.

The man with the black beard had recovered and risen. He and Sir Henry kept shaking hands with each other without a word to say.

Sir Henry said at last, "I thought you were dead. I have been over the Suliman Mountains to find you."

"I tried to go over the Suliman Mountains nearly two years ago," was the answer, spoken in the strange voice of a man who has had few opportunities recently to use his tongue, "but a rock fell on my leg and broke it, and I have been able neither to go forward nor to go back."

Then I came up. "How are you, Mr Neville?" I said. "Do you remember me?"

"Why," he said, "isn't it Quatermain, eh – and Good too? Hold on a minute, you fellows, I'm feeling faint again.

Sir Henry's brother comes out of his hut

It is all so very strange, and, when a man has ceased to hope, so very happy."

That evening over the camp-fire George Curtis told us his story. He had heard from local people that this was the best direction from which to approach the Suliman Mountains. They suffered a lot in crossing the desert. Finally, just as they reached this place, a terrible accident happened to George Curtis. When he was climbing, a great rock fell on his leg, breaking it to pieces, so that he found it impossible to go forward or back, and preferred to take the chance of living there where he had built his hut than the certainty of dying in the desert.

"And so," George Curtis ended, "we have lived for nearly two years like a second Robinson Crusoe and his man Friday, hoping that somebody might come here to help us away; but nobody has come. And now you appear! I thought that you had long ago forgotten about me and were living comfortably in England. But you appear, and find me where you least expected. It is the most wonderful thing I ever heard of!"

Our journey across the desert was very difficult, especially as we had to support George Curtis, whose right leg was very weak. But we did it somehow. To tell about the journey would only be to repeat much of what happened to us the time before.

Six months later we were safe at my little house near Durban, where I am now writing.

Just as I had written this last word, a postman came up the path carrying a letter. It was from Sir Henry Curtis, and I give it in full:

1 October 1884

My dear Quatermain,

I sent you a letter a few weeks ago to say that the three of us, George, Good and myself, reached England all right.

We went up to London together. You should have seen Good the next day – beautiful new clothes, beautiful new eyeglass.

To come to money matters – Good and I took the diamonds to Streeter's to find out what their real value was. Really I'm afraid to tell you what they told us: it seems such a huge amount. They advised us to sell a few at a time, as we shall get a better price in that way. They offered a hundred and eighty thousand pounds for just a few of the stones.

I want you to come home, dear old friend, and buy a house near here. You have done your day's work and have plenty of money now. There is a house that you can buy quite close here, which will suit you excellently. Do come. If you start immediately, you will be home by Christmas, and you must promise to stay with me for that.

Goodbye, old boy; I can't say more, but I know that you will come, if it is only to please

Your friend,

Henry Curtis

The axe with which I cut off Twala's head is fixed above my writing-table. I wish we could have brought away the coats of chain armour.

HC

Today is Tuesday. There is a ship going on Friday. I really think I must do as Curtis says.

Questions

Questions on each chapter

1 1 Where did Quatermain meet José Silvestre?
    2 Where did Quatermain meet Sir Henry Curtis?
    3 Where did Quatermain meet Neville?
    4 What did Neville set out to find?
    5 What did Sir Henry ask Quatermain to do?

2 1 Where and when had Quatermain seen Umbopa before?
      (At ... on ...)
    2 What did Umbopa want to do?
    3 Who agreed to take him?

3 1 How far was Sitanda's Kraal from Durban?
    2 How did they travel at first?
    3 How did they travel after that?
    4 What happened to Khiva?
    5 What could they see from Sitanda's Kraal?

4 1 What map did they have?
    2 How far did they march across the desert on the first
      night?
    3 How could they see to march by night?

5 1 Who said he could smell water?
    2 Why did they sit close together in the cave? (Because ...)
    3 What was the cause of Ventvogel's death?
    4 Whose was the other body?
    5 How long had the body been there?

6 1 What food was there on the other side of the mountain?
    2 What road did they find?
    3 Who threw a spear at Good?
    4 Who was "Him-whose-teeth-come-and-go"?

7   1   What would Ignosi be if he was alive?
      2   What was the meaning of "Koom"?
      3   Who was the commander of the Greys?

8   1   What happened to the soldier who dropped his shield?
      2   What did Twala first want Quatermain to kill?
      3   Who shot the elephant?
      4   Why did the king think that he ought to kill the white men? (Because ...)

9   1   What happens if a witch "smells out" a man?
      2   Why don't the people get rid of Twala?
      3   How many witches were there besides Gagool?
      4   Who was Umbopa touched by?

10   1   What did the chiefs want to see?
      2   Where did Infadoos take the four men?

11   1   Who made the plan for the battle?
      2   What was Sir Henry's place for the battle?
      3   Which company did Twala's army have to attack first?
      4   Who fought Twala himself?

12   1   What was the "Place of Death"?
      2   Why had Ignosi not killed Gagool? (So that ...)
      3   What was the huge hole in the ground?
      4   What were the "Silent Ones"?
      5   Where was Twala's body?

13   1   Where was the door of the treasure room?
      2   Who had dropped the goat-skin bag of diamonds?
      3   What were in the stone chests?
      4   What happened to Gagool?

14   1   Who noticed that the air stayed fresh?
      2   Who found the place the air was coming from?
      3   What did they use the last match for?
      4   Where did they come out of the last passage?

15   1   Where was Neville's hut?
      2   Why was Neville there? (Because ...)
      3   When he had read Sir Henry's letter, what did Quatermain decide to do?

Questions on the whole story

These are harder questions. Read the Introduction, and think hard about the questions before you answer them. Some of them ask for your opinion, and there is no fixed answer.

1   Who is the narrator (the person who is supposed to be telling the story)?

2   What do you know about the narrator's
    a   knowledge of southern Africa?
    b   skill as a hunter?
    c   knowledge of local languages?

3   Sir Henry Curtis:
    a   Why had he come to Africa?
    b   Where was his home?
    c   Can you describe his appearance?
    d   What do we know about his courage? Give examples.
    e   What do we know about his character?

4   Umbopa:
    a   Can you describe his appearance?
    b   What do we know about his courage? Give examples.
    c   What do we know about his character?
    d   What happened to him as a child?
    e   What did he become in the end?

5   Captain John Good:
    a   What do we know about his life before this story begins?
    b   Can you describe his appearance?
    c   What do we know about his character?

6   Gagool:
    a   How do you think she knew so much?
    b   Why do you think she had so much power?
    c   What happened to her in the end?

7   Sir H Rider Haggard:
    a   What is your opinion of him as a story-teller?
    b   Is there anything you don't like about his writing?
    c   How would you change the story for a film or television story for today?

New words

barrister
a lawyer who represents one side or the other in a court of law

classic
a work of art (writing, etc) that will always be considered good

committee
a small number of people appointed to consider some subject and report on it

eyeglass
a single piece of glass made to help a person with poor sight in one eye

false teeth
teeth that are not a person's natural teeth

fiction
stories about things that did not really happen

forehead
the part of the face above the eyes

kraal
(in southern Africa) a group of huts enclosed by a fence

Robinson Crusoe
a novel written in 1719 by Daniel Defoe. In the story Crusoe, alone on an island, saves an islander from death, and the man (Friday) becomes his servant.

rural
of the country (not towns)

vanish
disappear

wagon
a big, strong cart

witch
a woman who has (or is believed to have) magic powers